L1 44

C7D

The New Adventures of Postman Pat

Postman Pat™

takes flight

John Cunliffe
Illustrated by Stuart Trotter
from the original television designs by Ivor Wood

Hodder
Children's
Books

a division of Hodder Headline plc

More Postman Pat adventures:

Postman Pat and the big surprise
Postman Pat paints the ceiling
Postman Pat has too many parcels

First published 1997
by Hodder Children's Books,
a division of Hodder Headline plc,
338 Euston Road, London NW1 3BH

Story copyright © 1997 Ivor Wood and John Cunliffe
Text copyright © 1997 John Cunliffe
Illustrations copyright © 1997 Hodder Children's Books
and Woodland Animations Ltd.

ISBN 0 340 67815 1
10 9 8 7 6 5 4 3 2 1

Printed in Italy.

It was time for the post to be on its way in Greendale.
"Now then, Jess, let's be off!" said Pat.

The Greendale roads seemed more twisty and twiny than ever. Sometimes Pat wished he could fly like a bird and pop the letters and parcels down people's chimneys, like Father Christmas!

"Just fancy, Jess," said Pat. "Floating up in the sky, like a bird!"

The Reverend Timms was looking out for Pat.

"Oh, I'm so glad you're in good time," he said. "Oh, dear me, what a rush!"

"What's the hurry, Reverend?" said Pat.

"It's all to do with Mr Pringle and the Major," said the Reverend Timms. "Always at the last minute, bless us all! It's this film show they're giving. It has to be fitted in before the Major goes off to Timbuktu, can you believe? I never knew such a rush and a pother! All about flying, in that contraption of his. . ."

"Not that balloon I've heard tell about?" said Pat.

"Yes, that's it!" said the Reverend Timms.

"I'd love to see it!" said Pat.

"All welcome! Bring Sara and Julian! The more the better! Day after tomorrow! The thing is. . . there's not much time to tell people."

"Oh, I'll tell everybody!" said Pat. "I see most folks on my rounds."

"That's kind, Pat. And, if you could give them a leaflet as well. . . Miss Hubbard's running them off on that infernal machine of hers."

"She's my next call!" said Pat. "Two knitting-patterns and a tax-letter! I'll get a good stack of leaflets, don't you worry."

Pat was on his way.

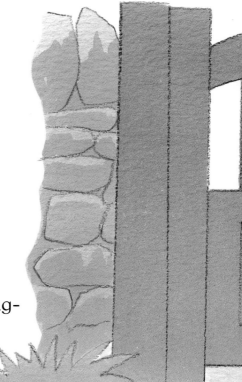

Miss Hubbard was glad to see him. "Oh, Pat, what a good thing you've come!" she said. "You're just in time to help. The copier's stopped right in the middle of printing these leaflets for. . ."

". . . the Major's film-show," said Pat, smiling.

"Oh. . . so you know," said Miss Hubbard. "Well, there's not a minute to lose; it's all in a rush, so, if you could wave your magic wand. . ."

"I wish I had one!" said Pat. "Never mind, let's have a look. . . There's nothing to these copiers. . ."

Pat lifted the lid, and poked at all the buttons and lights that he could see. He pulled and pushed and twiddled and fiddled. A large panel came loose, and a solid piece of the machine slid out and went *thump* on the carpet.

"Ooops!" said Pat. "It came off in my hands!"

"Oh, Pat, do take care!" said Miss Hubbard.

There was rather a lot of black powder on the carpet. When Pat picked the thing up, the black stuff went all over his hands, and his trousers, his face and his hair. It went just everywhere!

"It's a bit mucky, isn't it?" said Pat. "You wouldn't think there'd be so much in it!"

He pushed all the parts together, somehow, and switched the copier on. There was a whining and squealing, and a bright light came on.

"There you are! It's working!" he said.

He pushed a pile of paper into it, and pressed a button. It began to wheeze and cough, and groan and growl, and some very smeary and crumpled copies came out at the other end.

"Sounds a bit rough! Never mind, it's churning *something* out."

"It *is* rather smudgy," said Miss Hubbard, looking very doubtful.

"Never you mind that," said Pat. "They'll read it all right. I'll *tell* them the bits they can't read. Best be on my way, and get these delivered with the letters. Cheerio!"

His next stop was at Thompson Ground.

"Morning, Pat!" called Alf and Dorothy, from the yard.

"Morning, everybody!"

"A mucky one, if you ask me!" said Alf. "I wish you'd told us you were sweeping chimneys in your spare time. . . we have half a dozen need a good sweeping!"

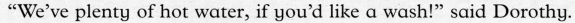

"We've plenty of hot water, if you'd like a wash!" said Dorothy.

"Nay, there's no time for that, with all this post to deliver, and these leaflets on top! It's all about the Major's film-show - with shots of his famous balloon! You can't miss it!"

Dorothy read it eagerly. "Oooh, yes, we'll come, all right!"

"So long as we don't get mucky faces like yours, Pat!" Alf said.

"Nay, you'll not do that! It's going to be a really good show! Bye!"

Pat was on his way. He handed out the leaflets wherever he went.
They seemed to get more and more smeary as time went on.

The day of the film-show came. The school hall was full, and the film was ready to show, but there was no sign of Major Forbes.

The Reverend Timms was pacing about outside, looking out for him. "Oh, I knew the Major would be late. . ." he fretted.

"Have you seen the Major, Pat?"

"Not a whisker!" said Pat.

"Did I tell you about the surprise?"

"Surprise, Reverend? No!"

"Yes, the Major promised there would be a big surprise! But where is he?"

"Tell you what," said Pat. "I'll pop up to Garner Hall and see if he needs a hand with anything. Won't be long."

At Garner Hall there was scaffolding all up one side, but no sign of the Major. Pat heard a sound from the sky.

"Hello," he called. "Who's that? *Where are you?*"

A long ladder led up towards the roof.
"He can't be up here, can he?" said Pat.

"Pat! Hi, Pat! Up here!"

It was the voice of Major Forbes, coming, again, from the sky. And then Pat saw him, drifting just above the chimneys, leaning out of a basket, that dangled under the biggest balloon Pat had ever seen.

"It's my jolly old anchor-rope. . . mixed up with the chimneys, *what*!" the Major shouted. "Be a good fellow, Pat: climb up and catch hold. . . see if you can cast me off!"

"I haven't much of a head for heights, Major, but, well, I'll have a go. . ."

Pat was terrified of that long ladder, and the ground seemed such a long way away when he reached the top.
"Ooooh, errrr, I don't like this!"

The major leaned dangerously out of his basket, and shouted directions to Pat. "There it is, Pat: catch hold and give it a good pull!"

Pat had to climb amongst the chimneys to reach the rope. He found the place where it was stuck fast, and pulled as hard as he could. He held on to the basket to keep himself from falling. The rope came free.

"Anchors away!" Pat shouted, but he found that the chimney was *going away from him*!

"Hey up, where's it going? Come back!"

He clung on to the basket.

"Sorry, Pat - can't stop!" the Major shouted. "Just hang on for dear life! I'll haul you in in just a jiffy! Heave ho! Don't let go!"

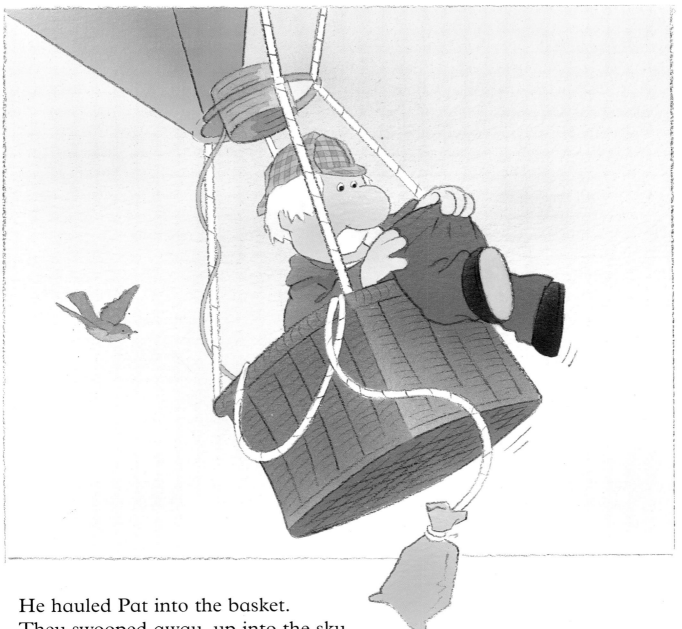

He hauled Pat into the basket.
They swooped away, up into the sky.

    "Late already, you know! Soon be there, with a following wind!"
the Major laughed.

    "Not to Timbuktu, I hope?" said Pat.

    "No. . . the school hall, of course!"

Pat had such a view of Greendale as he had never dreamed of. The hills and valleys drifted below them like a huge map. Roads wriggled away into the distance, with little cars on them that looked like toys. Far away, he could see the church in Pencaster. Still further, he saw the gleam of the sea. He was sad when it was time to land.

And what a surprise everyone had, when Pat and the Major came floating down in the balloon, and landed in the field next to the school! The children cheered!

The Reverend Timms said, "Well, Lord be praised, they've dropped out of the sky, safe and sound!"

"I could never have done it without Pat!" said Major Forbes. "It was those stupid chimneys of mine. Let's all go in and see the film!"

So they did.

Major Forbes showed them the films he had made when he flew his balloon across Africa.

"I saw elephants and lions there," he said, "but I never got my rope stuck round a chimney. . . !"

That night, Pat dreamed that he was a flying postman,
dropping letters and parcels down the chimneys of Greendale, or into
outstretched hands and aprons, through open windows, or on to soft
meadow grasses.

The next day he told Mrs Goggins about his dream.

"Oh, Pat!" she said. "A flying postman? That would never do. You might drop someone's parcel in a cow-pat!"

Pat laughed. "I suppose you're right! I'd better stick to my good old van!"